"Teller's reimagined tale . . . stands out among the best. . . . Fairy-tale aficionados will adore Teller's complex, touching retelling of this classic story of womanhood, perseverance, and familial love, in which she strikes an ideal balance between familiar and fresh."

—*Booklist* (starred review)

"A fascinating reimagining of the original tale. . . . Readers will feel empathy for Agnes, consider various misunderstandings, and think twice before labeling her as wicked."

—Lisa Ko, author of *The Leavers*

"As in the best literary inversions (e.g., Gregory Maguire's *Wicked*), Teller demonstrates the flaws and fine points of characters on both sides."

—*Washington Post*

"[A] charmed debut. . . . Teller pulls off the spellbinding trick of turning an easy-to-hate character into a strong and conscientious female lead."

—*Publishers Weekly*

"Sometimes you've only heard one part of the story. Cinderella's famously maligned stepmother, Agnes, gets to tell her own side in this clever take on the fairy tale, beginning as an impoverished laundress and eventually becoming the improbable lady of a manor and stepmom to a difficult little girl named Ella."

—*New York Post*

"Wonderfully elegant in its medieval manners and aristocratic language. With that courtliness as background, Teller woos readers into taking a better, more open-eyed look at a character that's been maligned for centuries, one with strength and who's worthy of stunned sympathy. . . . *All the Ever Afters* is one classy take on an old classic and is hard to put down, once started."

—*Guam Daily Post*

"Teller set aside an established medical career as a pulmonary doctor and researcher five years ago to write full time. Nevertheless, she plays surgeon still, extracting the (formerly) villainous stepmother as protagonist and skillfully excising the classic story's myths, magic and misconceptions."

—*San Jose Mercury News*

"Teller's novel is a powerfully written rendition of the Cinderella story. . . . Tells a complex tale of a love that forms through patient nurturing and by just being present." —Book Club Babble

ALL

THE

EVER

AFTERS

ALL
THE
EVER
AFTERS

The Untold Story of Cinderella's Stepmother

Danielle Teller

WILLIAM MORROW
An Imprint of HarperCollins Publishers

P.S.™ is a trademark of HarperCollins Publishers.

ALL THE EVER AFTERS. Copyright © 2018 by Danielle Teller. All rights reserved. Printed in the United States of America. No part of this book may be used or reproduced in any manner whatsoever without written permission except in the case of brief quotations embodied in critical articles and reviews. For information address HarperCollins Publishers, 195 Broadway, New York, NY 10007.

HarperCollins books may be purchased for educational, business, or sales promotional use. For information please e-mail the Special Markets Department at SPsales@harpercollins.com.

A hardcover edition of this book was published in 2018 by William Morrow, an imprint of HarperCollins Publishers.

FIRST WILLIAM MORROW PAPERBACK EDITION PUBLISHED 2019.

Designed by Leah Carlson-Stanisic

Borders created by Leah Carlson-Stanisic from artwork by Jamie Ekans/Shutterstock, Inc.

The Library of Congress has catalogued a previous edition as follows:

Names: Teller, Danielle, author.
Title: All the ever afters : the untold story of Cinderella's stepmother / Danielle Teller.
Description: First edition. | New York, NY : William Morrow, 2018.
Identifiers: LCCN 2017043121| ISBN 9780062798206 (hardback) | ISBN 9780062798077 (trade pb)
Subjects: LCSH: Cinderella (Tale)—Adaptations. | Stepmothers—Fiction. | BISAC: FICTION / Fairy Tales, Folk Tales, Legends & Mythology. | FICTION / Historical. | FICTION / Literary.
Classification: LCC PS3620.E447 A79 2018 | DDC 813/.6—dc23
LC record available at https://lccn.loc.gov/2017043121

ISBN 978-0-06-279807-7 (pbk.)

19 20 21 22 23   10 9 8 7 6 5 4 3 2 1

In memory of Anne Shreenan Dyck,
the best mom in the whole world

ALL

THE

EVER

AFTERS

Prologue

THE ROYAL COURT

Suppers at the royal court have become entirely too oppressive. It isn't just that they are interminable, or that we must adhere to the newest fashions, the face powder, our hair tortured into great bejeweled rams' horns, the silks with sleeves so tight that it's impossible to raise one's spoon to one's carefully tinctured lips— No, the worst is the gossip, the sinister buzz of wasps ready to slip their poisonous stingers into whatever tender flesh lies exposed.

This evening I was ordered to sit next to the Earl of Bryston, a pompous halfwit who has rarely been to court. He presides over some godforsaken swamp in the north, and he seems to believe that his family's long history of loyalty to the crown gives him the right to opine on the behaviors of the royal family.

"My lady," he said, plucking at cuffs so voluminous that they draped into his soup, "I understand that your noble daughters are not yet wed?"

"No, my lord," I answered as briefly as courtesy would allow.

"And yet, I have heard that they once vied for the attention of

Prince Henry himself?" The earl dabbed his crimson lips daintily. "That they tried to alienate his affection from Princess Elfilda?"

"You seem amused, my lord." He could not have mistaken the coldness in my response. "I fear that much of what you have heard is not true."

"Ah, well, it is an incredible tale!" He smiled broadly. "The beautiful downtrodden maiden who ascends to the royal palace, the jealous stepsisters, the glass slipper that would not fit . . ."

"My lord, I cannot credit such a tale."

"Come, my lady! You know that the whole kingdom is enthralled by our radiant and benevolent princess! I have heard a great deal about you and your daughters." He looked at me knowingly.

"Compelling fiction often obscures the humble truth."

"I do hope that you will tell me about the slipper," he said, ignoring my reluctance. He broke a piece of bread, leaving a trail of crumbs across the table. "My wife is frantic to know the particulars! They say that the prince let every maiden try the shoe, even your daughters!" He laughed.

"It is droll to imagine them receiving attention from a prince?"

"Well . . ." His shrug was eloquent.

"They are ugly, and Elfilda is beautiful."

The earl frowned and pursed his lips. It is genteel to imply nasty insults, not to speak them directly.

"My lord, I may have heard some of the rumors to which you allude. To my mind, these stories insinuate a plague of blindness. Prince Henry would have to be blind not to recognize the object of his admiration or to distinguish an ugly girl from one of unsurpassed beauty. My daughters would need to be blind to their reflections in mirrors and on the faces of those who behold them—" My voice rose, so I paused and began again blandly. "They would also need to be blind to the truth that men persuade themselves that beautiful women possess virtue and good character, whereas no amount of virtue can make an ugly woman beautiful."

"My lady, Princess Elfilda is a dazzling star who shines in the royal firmament, where she belongs." He did not attempt to conceal his disdain. "That she invites you and your daughters to dine here at the palace is a testament to her compassion, forgiveness, and generosity."

"Indeed, my lord," I murmured. "Indeed that is so."

I am only of interest to the Earl of Bryston and his ilk because of my stepdaughter. Princess Elfilda is the most celebrated woman in the kingdom, perhaps in all of history. Commoners line the streets for endless hours, even in dark and sleet, hoping to glimpse her face through the window of her gilded carriage. When the princess has her gown cut in a new way or adopts a different hairstyle, every female creature in the city imitates her appearance. Last autumn she wore a choker of pearls to church on Michaelmas, and the next day every noblewoman's throat was wound snugly with pearls or other jewels. By Christmastide even the peasant girls wore chokers of beads or ribbon, whatever material they could find to replicate the fashion.

Princess Elfilda's popularity derives in large part from her astonishing beauty, but there is something else about her nature that attracts the masses. Her habitual muteness and the gentle hesitancy of those rare words that do fall from her lips make her seem bashful, as does her manner of ducking her head and looking up through sweeping lashes. Apart from her collections of baubles and kennel of favorite dogs, she appears to have no passions or vices, and when she attends royal functions, her gaze drifts to invisible spectacles that only she can apprehend. Her elusive character is a blank parchment upon which any story may be written, and every girl who dreams of becoming a princess can imagine herself in Princess Elfilda's famously tiny shoes.

I know more of the princess's history than anyone else alive, and the true tale is not as fantastical as the one sung by troubadours. Nobody is interested in the story of a flesh-and-blood nobleman's daughter, one who wet her bed, complained of boredom, fought with her kin, and turned up her nose at winter greens just like any mortal child. Nor do I have any desire to diminish the adulation for the princess, which makes both the admiring and admired so content.

I do not set out to write the princess's history, but my own, the only tale I have the authority to tell. My quill may resurrect ghosts to keep me company during the long days at the castle, and if it cannot, at least my mind will be occupied and my hands busy. As for fables about good and evil and songs about glass slippers, I shall leave those to the minstrels. They can invent their own tales about Cinderella.

THE MANOR HOUSE

I hardly remember my own mother. I have a memory of arms surrounding me and pushing my head into a soft bosom that smelled of kitchen smoke, lye, and some light acrid scent that I can no longer identify. This memory evokes comfort, but also childish impatience and distaste for yielding flesh.

I do remember her singing; she had a pretty voice. She had heavy auburn hair that she would sometimes allow me to braid.

I was told that she died in agony while my brother tried and failed to enter this world. She labored for three long days as the baby died inside her. Then she too was called to God's side. I do not know where I was as she lay those three days on the birthing bed that became her deathbed. Maybe I was sent away to a neighboring home. Maybe my mind recoiled so violently at the scene of her death that the memory ripped free. I wonder sometimes if the thoughts that flock my nightmares are abandoned memories coming home to roost.

Several years after my mother died, I was sent to work at the manor house. I would have been sent there eventually, because my

father was only a half-virgater, poorer than most, and I was the
youngest of three children. My brother and my father did what
they could with our land, but they also owed work in other parts
of the manor's holdings. I was certainly not going to have a dowry,
and there was no need for two girls to tend to our cottage. Under
more fortunate circumstances, I might have remained at home several years longer to help my mother with the baby, but as it was, I
left home with half of my milk teeth. I was a sturdy child, big for
my age and strong. My father must have believed that I would fare
well at the manor house.

On the day I was to leave home, I lay in the loft long after everyone else had risen. I kept my eyes shut, listening as my sister made
the fire and chided the hens that got in her way.

My father said, "You should wake Agnes." Still, I did not move.

"Agnes!" my sister scolded. "Get up and say good-bye to Father and Thomas!" Reluctantly, I rose and lowered myself from
the loft. My father's gaze was grave but unapologetic. He opened
his arms to signal that he wished me to approach and embrace him.

"Remember that your mother will be watching from heaven,"
he said gruffly. "Be godly and good. We shall see you on May
Day." He released me and turned toward the door.

"Bye, Nessie," my brother said softly, "we shall miss you."

I watched them dissolve into the morning twilight mist as they
left to harness the oxen.

"Let's get you a warm bowl of pottage before you go," my sister said. She stirred the steaming pot on the hearth briskly. When
she looked up, tears glistened in her eyes. "Oh, this green wood
smokes too much," she said. "It makes my eyes sting."

The walk from our cottage in Over End to the church in Nether

End was as familiar as a lullaby, but I had never been beyond the church. The crouching woods of Aviceford Manor's demesne lay beyond the river that divided the church from the manor's holdings. On the Sabbath, it was my habit to steal a moment before Mass to visit the riverbank, where I would scour the sand for pretty stones. Even in winter, as long as the snow was not too deep, I would risk a scolding to slip over the embankment. Once near the river, however, I cast only a rare glance into the dark underbrush on the far bank. I knew of fairies who dwelt in rotting mossy trunks, fairies who stole babies from hearthsides at night and left changelings in their places. I was too big for the fairies to snatch, but I did not care to glimpse a scurrying shadow in the woods, sly yellow eyes gleaming.

Once safely inside the church, I would sit beneath a high lancet window facing the trees, holding a smooth stone in my hand and following the dance of dust motes animated by wavering sunlight. There I would remember that fairies are not real.

On that day in early spring, the swollen river swallowed the banks nearly whole, and bare branches scratched at low clouds. Though it had rained heavily the night before, the sky still hung close and dark, pregnant with water. It settled itself over me, making it difficult to breathe.

I counted twenty-two wet logs beneath my feet as I crossed the slippery bridge. Once on the other side, entering the mouth of the forest, my breath eased a little. The trees on either side were quite ordinary, and the wet road remained familiar underfoot. The mud sucked greedily, pulling a shoe right off, and my stockinged foot squelched deep into the muck. After that, much to my irritation, my shoe slipped from my slick foot every time my attention wandered.

I carried with me a small bag containing my other gown, my cloak, the wooden cross my father had made for me, warm stockings my sister had mended, and my collection of stones. Stones are a foolish thing to carry through the countryside, but I was attached to my collection, which I had curated over the course of years. For every stone that I kept, I rejected twenty. Each had to be unique, and it had to harmonize with the others in the collection besides. My favorite place to hunt for stones was at the river, where the water wore them smooth, and the damp brought out color and patterns in the rock. My most treasured stone was oval and flat like a flagstone. The green face was shot through with gold lines, like silken threads in a tapestry. I would hold that stone in the palm of my hand to soothe myself when I had trouble sleeping at night.

Where the woods thinned, yellow coltsfoot pushed through dead grass and leaves, the coarse, genial blooms undimmed by midday blackness. The woods gave way to meadowland, and as the road began to climb, orchards. I knew that my father sometimes worked in these orchards and nearby fields, and I marveled at the distance he had to travel for his week-work.

I struggled to keep my shoe on my foot as I climbed toward the manor house, and this distracted me enough that the appearance of a gate in front of me took me by surprise. I had expected a grand building, but I was unprepared for the scale of the surrounding wall. The wooden gate was reinforced with bands and studs of iron, and it stood at least twice as high and three times as wide as the doors of the church. To my relief, the gate rested ajar, and I pushed with my shoulder to open it farther.

The stench of pigs was first to greet me, and then the confusing sight of several squat structures, some of wood and some of stone. The ponderous sky chose that moment to release its burden; thick sheets of rain obscured my view and battered me with fat, tiny fists. I ran to the nearest building to escape, realizing as I approached that it was a stable. If the horses objected to my intrusion, their noise was drowned by the hammering of rain on the slate roof.

I huddled in a corner, away from the draught, watching the drops gather and fall from the ends of my hair, yearning for our warm hearth and my sister's chatter. I would only be allowed to leave the manor on saints' days and other holidays, and I would never again wake up snug against my sister's warm back. A prickling behind my eyes and tightness in my throat told me to think of other things. I could make out the glossy flanks of horses in the dim light; sometimes a shadowy eye gleamed over the edge of a stall. The air was pungent, but I was comforted by the smell, which I associated with the warmth of their sturdy bodies. I never learned to ride, but I think that I would have enjoyed it.

I never understood why Elfilda—Ella, we called her then, before she became a princess—was so afraid of horses. Her father insisted that she learn to ride. At some point, it was left to me to enforce this dictate. Ella fought the poor stableboy like a cat when he tried to lift her onto the back of a palfrey. When I took the reins and slapped her pale hands sharply, she desisted long enough for the boy to lead her on a slow walk. She never did learn to ride properly, however. It is probably just as well, since hawking makes her cry for the dead bunnies, and hunting is even worse. When the royal court hunts, she feigns illness, though by now her husband must have realized that she will never join them. She takes refuge with her dogs in the kennel, or with us, until the horses are stabled and the meat hung out of sight.

When the rain slowed, I made my way back outside. The sky had brightened a little, and I took in the scene around me. I could see now that there were two gates, the one I had passed through and a second gate farther on, surrounded by tall hedges. Over the hedges, I could make out what I assumed to be the roof of the manor house.

The gate swung briskly open, and a man and a boy appeared. I had not passed a single soul on the road, and I was pleased to see two of my own kind. They wore plain jerkins and hats to shade their faces, and the boy carried a gardener's scythe in his belt. I hastened toward them, my bag bouncing on my back.

The man turned his furrowed face, his pale eyes nearly vanishing beneath wrinkles when he smiled.

"Ho, missy!" He tipped his hat. "What brings a drowned mouse like you out of the woods?"

"My father heard from the bailiff that the manor house is in need of a new laundry girl."

"Is that so? And you think a wee girl like you will be useful to the laundress?"

"I am not small!" I pointed to the boy standing sulkily beside him. "I am taller than him!"

The man laughed. "True enough, true enough. Well, I don't know much about laundry, but it does not surprise me that Miss Elisabeth is in need of another new laundry girl. She has a sharp tongue, that one."

My heart sank again, but I said nothing.

"My name is John, and this here is Benedict. He is going to help me to prune some trees in the orchard, aren't you, Benedict my boy?" The boy scowled, and John jostled him. "You will have to excuse the bad manners of my young apprentice; he is an odd boy who does not like to climb trees. What might we call you, missy?"

"Agnes, sir."

"Well, Agnes, I am very pleased to meet you. If you run along to the house, the chamberlain will find Miss Elisabeth for you. Go to the back door, past the herb garden. That is the kitchen entrance, and someone there can point you to Mr. Geoffrey. If Mr. Geoffrey is in a good mood, he might let you have a spot of bacon and some ale while you dry out." John winked as he turned back toward the orchard. "Take what you can get when you can get it, Agnes, and you will fare all right here."

His parting comment did not settle my nerves, but the mention of bacon made my mouth water. The rain had stopped entirely. With a deep breath, I entered the gate through which John and Benedict had appeared and saw Aviceford Manor for the first time.

The sky continued to play games with me: The same moment that the house came into view, the sun leapt from behind a cloud, beaming sudden life into the red sandstone walls of the manor. Rows of glazed windows shone golden, diamond panes glinting. The only glass windows I knew were the narrow lancet windows at church; this house boasted grand mullioned windows, recessed under decorative arches. To my young eyes, the house might have been a castle. The massive main building was flanked by crenelated turrets, ornamented with three stories of lacey cusping and delicate, clover-shaped quatrefoil windows. Lion head corbels guarded the vaulted entrance; above them squatted fanciful spiky-eared gargoyles, their wide mouths holding trumpetlike water spouts.

I could not see the rats, scuttling in the shadows, or hear the crunching of termites, feasting on rafters and braces. I could not feel the ivy, ripping at stone, turning towers into sand. I knew nothing yet of the cloying sickness of relations in that house. To me, the manor was simply beautiful. I was, after all, a child.

THE LAUNDRY

For those unfamiliar with Aviceford Manor, it is the smallest of three manors that lie within the grand landholding of Ellis Abbey. The Abbess Elfilda (yes, the godmother of Princess Elfilda) appointed Emont Vis-de-Loup, youngest son of Lord Henry Vis-de-Loup, 4th Baron of Wilston, to act as manorial lord at Aviceford. Emont would inherit little from his family, and he could never hope to be a tenant-in-chief like his father, but the manor provided him with a comfortable living even after the abbey took its share.

Emont was unmarried, and gossipers in the village liked to say that he saved his affection for barrels of ale and bottles of wine. This shifted more than the usual burden of manorial supervision to the chamberlain. Geoffrey Poke had been well ensconced at the top of the servants' hierarchy when Emont became lord, and the combination of Geoffrey's craving for authority and Emont's disinterest allowed the chamberlain to expand the power of his position. By the time I met him, he had become an iron-fisted autocrat who did not brook even the most trifling opposition from his inferiors.

As I first stood before him in the hallway by the buttery, I might have been a disappointingly small wood pigeon he was considering having plucked for dinner. He slowly circled, examining me from my sodden hair to my humiliatingly exposed foot—I had been obliged to leave my muddy stocking outside along with my shoes.

Abruptly, he said, "What is your father's name, and where does he live?" His voice was thin and nasal.

"William, sir. William Rolfe. We live in Over End."

"Over End, Aviceford Village?"

"Yes, sir."

"What are you, fourteen years old?"

"Ten, sir. Nearly eleven."

He lifted his eyebrows. "What use are you?"

"I am a hard worker, sir. I am strong, and my mother taught me well."

"What would your mother know about laundry?" He brought his hatchet face close to mine. "You smell like pigs' dung."

I stared at his fat lower lip, peculiarly fleshy in his narrow face, glistening with spit. His mouth was so crowded with teeth that his lips did not fully close. I wanted to back away from his unpleasant breath.

Geoffrey continued to stare at me, moistening his lips again with his tongue. He made a grunting noise in the back of his throat. "I suppose you will do," he said finally, moving away. "The laundry has been piling up since the last girl left, and I am running out of linens. I shall take you to Elisabeth."

I had been thinking of bacon since my conversation with John. As the tall chamberlain led me away from the kitchen, I felt like a savory morsel had been snatched from my hand. "Sir?" I said. "I have had nothing to eat since daybreak."

He looked at me with irritation. "Dinner has already been cleared. If you are lucky, you might get some supper."

As we traversed a narrow passageway of stones, their surfaces cracked and rough as ancient cowhide, I noticed the chamberlain's awkward gait. The sole of his left shoe was several times the thickness of the right, and the blunt toe angled in a strange direction. What grotesque deformity hid beneath the oiled covering?

The hall tapered away in front of us into the gloom, disappearing into the black maw of an open doorway. Geoffrey jabbed a long finger toward the entrance. "There is the laundry room. Go find Elisabeth." He limped away, leaving me alone in the passage.

I peered from the doorway into darkness. Weak light from a solitary window near the ceiling illuminated a shallow, stone-lined pool of water on the floor, but the rest of the room lay in shadow. Gradually, the shadows assumed recognizable forms. An enormous wooden bucking tub squatted near the pool, raised on four stout feet. Along the back wall was a cold fireplace, ashes spilling over the edge of the hearth, wood strewn in disorderly piles. A mountain of linens towered in the corner. There was no laundress.

When I considered returning to the chamberlain, my stomach clenched sickeningly. I would wait for the laundress to return. I looked for a seat, and as there was none, I perched on a smooth stone at the lip of the pool. The stones formed a low wall around what presumably functioned as a laundry basin. I decided to put on my clean stockings while I waited. I was hungry and damp, but at least I would have warm feet.

As I bent forward to peel off my single wet stocking, a deep sighing breath broke the silence of the room, like a rock thrown into a still pond. I froze, the hairs rising on my arms.

A stirring in the heap of linens should have returned me to my senses, but instead, I panicked. I scrambled backward, splashing loudly into the slack pool. The water must have been standing unused for a great length of time to have accumulated such a thick layer of slime, and my disturbance released an evil stench. A shrill screech filled the room, echoing, as the laundress rose from the pile of soiled linens and bore down upon me.

"Get out of there!" Her massive bosom heaved. "Get out, you little brat! What are you doing?"

Slipping on the slime-covered stones, I did my best to oblige. "My name is Agnes, miss, and I am the new laundry girl."

The look she gave me was impenetrable. She placed incongruously doll-like hands on her ample hips. When she began again, her tone was measured. "If you are the new laundry girl, we had better see what you can do. Considering how much work you have," she jerked her head toward the pile of laundry, "you had better get started right away, hadn't you?"

"Yes, miss." I shivered. The room was cold, and I was dripping wet.

"It is cold in here, but lucky for you, your first job will be to build a fire." She stepped into the shaft of sunlight, and for the first time, I saw her properly. She was as plump as a Christmas goose; I marveled at her girth. Yellow curls escaped from the edge of her dirty bonnet. Her face might have been pretty if her delicate features had not been enfolded in doughy flesh. "What are you waiting for?" she asked sharply.

I hunched my shoulders and slid over to the fireplace to sweep the hearth, keeping my head down. Weeks' worth of ashes choked the fireplace. I filled the bucket with as many cinders as would fit, clearing some space, and I built a small bed for the fire using twigs and straw. Next to the fireplace, I found a good flint and a supply of char cloth, and the fire was soon lit. I then began to organize the haphazard piles of wood and kindling on the floor.

"Never mind that," said the laundress. "Get the ashes ready."

I looked at her, confused.

"Spread the ashes on the bucking cloth, you idiot!"

I had never used a bucking tub before. Gingerly, I reached up and sprinkled black soot on the cloth that stretched taut over the opening.

"Afraid of straining your wee delicate arms, princess? Dump those ashes and fetch water from the rain barrel." She handed me an ancient, blackened kettle.

My footsteps echoed dully as I retraced my steps through the narrow hallway, past the cramped and lightless buttery and into the back foyer. Late-afternoon sunlight streamed through the windows, dazzling my eyes and coalescing in bright pools on the flagstones. I could see that a coating of ashes clung to my wet frock; brushing at them only made dark smears.

As I approached the heavy doors of the kitchen, which hung ajar, an invisible wall of sound and scent—clanging pots, muffled shouts, the aroma of roasting chicken and baking bread—arrested my feet in midstride. I inhaled greedily, which only goaded my hunger into sinking its claws deeper.

Outside, my shoes were hardly drier than I had left them, but I knocked off the mud as best I could and put them back on. A path snaked along the rear wall of the manor, leading to the gardens and dovecote. As the stone slabs were slippery with rain and moss, I walked alongside, in the coarse and dripping seedling grasses, swinging the empty kettle to make raindrops scatter from drooping stalks of dogtail.

Over the low wall surrounding the herb garden, I recognized the back of John's leather jerkin and his frayed hat. He yanked up fistfuls of young mint and comfrey, which ran amok, covering the soil in a riotous froth of green. Doubtless he was beating the shoots back to make room for herbs that still slumbered in the earth.

"Little mouse!" he said with a laugh. "You have turned from a pretty little white mousie to a black one; did you meet a witch?"

I grimaced, and his smile softened.

"Cheer up, little mouse. Miss Elisabeth is hard-hearted, but she is a practical woman. You look like a clever girl who can find a way to work with her. Keep your chin up."

I nodded and carried on. Nothing was served by arguing.

A rain barrel was located at the far side of the herb garden, where it could be used for watering. I plunged the kettle deep into the clean, chill water. The cold was both painful and delicious, and I pushed my arms deeper, leaning against the barrel. Light rippled across the surface of the water, and as it calmed, I could see my reflection peering back at me. If my heart had not been so heavy, I would have laughed. My face was almost entirely black; only my serious brown eyes were recognizable to me. I released the kettle with one hand to splash water on my face.

John was nowhere to be seen as I struggled back toward the house, holding the kettle with both hands, trying to keep it from knocking against my shins. Once again, I paused at the entrance to the laundry room, allowing my eyes to adjust to the dimness.

The laundress had stretched herself out on the pile of dirty linens, and I hoped that she had fallen asleep. She stirred as soon as I entered the room, however, and sat up.

"What took you so long? You will not sleep tonight at this rate." She adjusted her cap primly. "Put the kettle on the fire. You will need to keep fetching water and heating it until the tub is full. If you are lucky, you might be done before the compline bell, but I doubt it." She rose, smoothing her skirt. "I am going to supper."

"But, miss, I have not eaten since daybreak!"

"Then you had better hurry." She crossed to the door with a surprisingly light step. "When you finish here, you will sleep in the kitchen. There will be a trundle next to the larder." Her shadow, which had eclipsed the doorway, disappeared.

I confess that I felt very sorry for myself in that moment. After she left, I sat by the fire and had a cry. It was the first time that I had been away from my family, and my sister's absence was a hole through my chest. I had never been thankful enough for Lottie's bowls of filling pottage, or for the comfort of nestling against her solid back, rocking with each sleeping breath. I yearned for home, but even as I watched my tears splash into the feathery ashes, I was aware of another feeling. Deep beneath my piteous thoughts curled something else, something hard and vengeful.

My arms tired from carrying loads of water and lifting the heavy kettle over the tub. Light faded and then departed from the window. Though it became more difficult to see, I did not much miss the cheerless light. The firelight was not enough, but it was hearty.

I was preoccupied when John came into the room, and I started when he coughed.

"Sorry, mousie, I did not mean to frighten you. I just brought you a little supper."

As he set a cloth-covered bundle and clay bottle on the floor, I had a giddy impulse to run to him and throw my arms around his narrow chest, like I used to do to my father when I was a tot. Instead, I said, "How can I thank you, sir?"

"Ah, Agnes, it's nothing. And everybody here calls me John. I saw Elisabeth in the kitchen and figured that you might be needing a bite of food to keep you going. I brought you some cold chicken with onion and a bit of bread, as well as a spot of ale. One thing you will like about working at the manor is the food!"

"God bless you, and thank you, thank you, thank you!"

He looked amused by my effusiveness. "I am going to bed. The menservants sleep in the outbuildings, but the laundress and laundry girl sleep in the kitchen."

"Miss Elisabeth said that there will be a pallet near the larder."

He must have heard my discouragement, for he sighed and said, "I came to the manor when I was near your age. Elisabeth was even younger. I remember how she ran away. Came back with a black eye and probably worse. Her father had too many mouths to feed. It can be hard here for a child, I grant you. Some people let it get to them. Don't you do that. You do your best to get by, and one day you will be head laundress, and you will have a laundry girl working for you."

His words were no comfort, but I said, "Yes, sir."

"Good night, Agnes."

"Good night, sir."

I fell on the tray when he left and ate with relish. Chicken was a rare treat; the food and John's kindness lifted my spirits. Though my arms were sore and my body drained, the remaining hours of work did not seem as onerous as the first. I kept my mind occupied with fantasies about manor food and the approach of May Day, when I would have the whole day free to celebrate at the parish church.

After banking the fire, I gathered my bag and made my way to the kitchen. The passageway was dark as pitch, but pale moonlight from windows in the back foyer guided me to the kitchen doors. The room appeared too grand to be a kitchen; its lofty height seemed more fitting for a cathedral. Shafts of moonlight illuminated lingering blue smoke near the vaulted ceiling. Scattered streaks from a skylight pierced the gently roiling smoke, like the Holy Ghost descending.

Embers glowed in a fireplace massive enough to contain a whole ox, silhouetting a heap of blankets on the floor that must have contained my new enemy. Even her bulk was dwarfed by the size of the hearthstone. She had told me to look for my bed by the larder, which I deduced was the dark entrance yawning in the back wall. It did not surprise me to see how far it was from the fire. I circled the trestle tables and found in one of their shadows the straw mat that the laundress had left for me. A thin blanket had been placed atop the pallet.

I removed my cloak and collection of stones from my bag, dropping the sac at one end of the mat for use as a pillow. Though I wanted to collapse from exhaustion, I first aligned my stones in a row across the head of my bed, a tiny wall of soldiers to guard me in my sleep. I then wrapped myself as well as I could in my cloak and blanket, and I sank into the sleep of the dead.

THE ROYAL COURT

Solitude is the commodity in shortest supply at the palace, but Princess Elfilda has succeeded in carving out a generous portion for herself. She has always been happiest in her own company. It pleases her to have familiar faces nearby, but she does not enjoy social intercourse. If she could do away with ladies-in-waiting entirely, she would, but as that is not possible, she has relegated them to a suite separate from her own. My daughters are among those ladies, and though their duties are light, they are not allowed to stray from the retinue. It pains me that I so seldom have the pleasure of their company.

Today is a joyful day, because they came walking with me, my daughters, Charlotte and Matilda. The king and queen have left for the summer palace, and with most of the royal family and courtiers absent, it feels like a holiday.

"Mother!" Matilda called when she found me in the nearly deserted garden; she ran to me and threw her arms around my shoulders in an enthusiastic embrace. Even as I staggered to keep my balance, I reveled in the solidity of her body, the vital warmth and heft of her precious flesh and blood and bones.

Charlotte followed in a more stately fashion, reproaching her sister. "You should never run, Tilly. Stop acting like a baby. God be with you, Mother." She kissed my cheek fondly. "You look lovely. This style suits you. Your waist is as tiny as a maiden's."

"And my brow is as wrinkled as an old crone's."

"Ha!" Matilda kissed my other cheek. "You are as fair as this spring day."

"If by fair you mean argent."

"You are insufferable, Mother," Matilda said. "There is hardly a gray hair on your head."

The girls each took one of my arms. They are both a fingersbreadth taller than me, broad shouldered and sturdy. They leaned in close and gripped tightly, ushering me down the path like a couple of palace guards removing an unruly petitioner from the throne room. The sensation was surprisingly pleasant; I floated through the garden on strong currents of their affection.

The palace grounds are impressive but austere. There are no flowers, only fancy topiaries, fountains, and statues. The groomed footpaths take straight lines and cross at sharp angles, their geometry unsoftened by shade and ungraced by the prolific disorder of nature. I feel exposed there, exposed to the harsh sun and to the many pairs of eyes that gaze from palace windows and passing coaches.

As we skirted the central fountain, the sun's rays burned through a straggling skein of cloud and spread a hard glitter over the onyx pool. We turned toward a side trail that meanders through a copse of trees, a corner of the grounds that had been allowed to retain a glimmer of the wild.

"It's such a relief to be rid of Lady Margaret," Matilda said. She referred to the mistress of the robes, an imperious woman who kept a strict watch over the ladies-in-waiting.

"Even Cinderella is more cheerful now that the shrew is away."

"You should refer to your stepsister as Princess Elfilda," I admonished, "and please don't let anyone hear you calling names. We have enough trouble."

Matilda stuck out her tongue and rolled her eyes comically. "Well, Lady Margaret is a shrew, and everyone knows it, including Princess Oblivious."

"Ella isn't oblivious," Charlotte said. "She just doesn't care about gossip and intrigue."

"*Princess* Ella to you."

This time it was Charlotte's turn to stick out her tongue at her sister.

"In any event," Matilda continued, "I didn't mean oblivious in the sense of stupid; we all know that she is quick-witted when it comes to lessons and music. I only meant that she wouldn't know a backstabber if she witnessed her wiping blood from a dagger on the back of a corpse."

"Exceedingly colorful image, dearheart. How worried ought I be?" I asked.

Charlotte sighed. "Nobody is in danger of being stabbed with a dagger. Tilly is being dramatic. It is only that everybody wants something. Cecily Barrett's fine bosom is on display for Prince Henry at every possible opportunity, and he can't help but feast his eyes——and who knows what else. Ella——pardon me, Princess

Elfilda——is so innocent, she doesn't even notice; she has chosen Cecily as her favorite because she takes an interest in the dogs. Cecily doesn't give a fig about dogs. She only pretends to care to gain some advantage."

"Cecily isn't even as bad as some of the others," Matilda said. "That Hamelin girl has got her sticky fingers in the coffer. She buys clothing and collectables for Ella, who has no idea about the price of goods. Then she wonders why her allowance is all used up halfway through the year."

"What about you?" I asked. "Has the situation improved at all?"

Charlotte pulled me closer and planted another kiss on my cheek. "Don't fret about us, sweet Mother. We are so fortunate to be here."

We walked in silence for a few moments. The dappled shade of trees gave us relief from the glare of sun and afforded us temporary privacy. Long shadows of trunks banded the path ahead with shades of dove gray and gold.

"I can't help but worry," I said. "I hear whispers about you."

"They are nothing more than that. Whispers."

"Oh, but you must tell Mother about your great toe!" Matilda said with bitter amusement.

"Do hold your tongue, Tilly!"

"What is this about your toe?"

"Nothing, idle gossip," Charlotte said.

"Come on, tell her!"

"You tell her if you are so eager! You are such a troublemaker."

"Well, the other day several of the ladies cornered us and insisted that we remove our shoes," Matilda said. "'Whatever for?' we asked. 'We have heard that you are missing parts of your feet,' they replied. I thought they were daft. But they told us there's a story circulating about Prince Henry using Ella's abandoned little shoe to track her down after she ran away from the ball. They said that Lottie and I pretended to be Ella. Both of us! Hoping that he would marry one of us." Matilda laughed, and I felt Charlotte flinch. "They said Lottie was so convinced the prince would mistake her for Ella that she cut off her great toe to fit into the slipper. And when she failed, I decided that it would be an excellent idea to cut off my heel and shove my mangled foot into the bloody shoe, sure that Prince Henry would look at me and say, 'You are the beautiful creature I danced with all last night!'" Matilda's voice had grown thick with the threat of tears, and she ended with a little gasp that was halfway between a laugh and a sob.

Charlotte gripped my arm with all of the ferocity that she kept from her voice. "We mustn't repeat such nonsense, Tilly. We should just be grateful that our stepsister married well and that we are here."

"But who would make up such scandalous lies?" Helplessness drove the claws of my anger inward. I wanted to make myself a living barrier between those vile women and my daughters, to protect them as I could when they were children.

"It is merely the way rumors grow," Charlotte said, stroking my back. "These ladies ingratiate themselves with Ella, and they wheedle for bitty morsels of gossip. She means no harm. You know how Ella is; she reports the particulars faithfully without always understanding the larger picture. Remember when she was a wee girl, and she told us that Frère Joachim had brought a whip to punish her if she was naughty? You were furious, but it turned out that the 'whip' was only a bulrush that he had brought inside for his lesson. Ella didn't understand that he was jesting. I suppose she had never seen a real whip."

Indeed, I am sure that Princess Elfilda has not seen a whip or a switch to this day. Children of noblemen are not casually beaten in the way that is so customary for poor children.

THE LORD OF THE MANOR

On my second day at the manor, I woke to the sound of men bickering. Three pairs of legs clad in rough woolen stockings were visible to me under the table; these belonged to kitchen scullions engaged in a heated argument over who would split the wood and who would set the fire. I squinted into the bright sunlight and stood up gingerly. I had overslept. My back and arms ached, and the cold had seeped into my bones. I would need a thicker blanket if I was going to continue to sleep alone and so far from the fire.

The scullions paid me no heed. One gestured emphatically as he made his case, slicing through interruptions with sharp chopping motions. A much older scullion leaned listlessly on the table, a passive expression on his face. It was disgraceful that the boys would not give the older man the lightest task. He looked as though he might be ill.

The laundress was nowhere in sight, and her bedding had been removed. I wondered why she had not woken me. It was surely not out of kindness that she let me sleep.

I put my two favorite stones in my pocket and returned the re-

mainder to the sac along with my cloak; I then looked in the larder
for a place to store my bedding. The room was windowless and
dank. Appetizing and rancid smells mingled to create an aroma
that befuddled the nose and stomach. Two thick slabs of meat dangled from the ceiling, and a side of beef lay bleeding on a broad
stone thrall. The shelves held crocks of lumpish gray meat bur-
ied in gelatinous lard, meat that one day would dance and sizzle
deliciously over the fire after its heavy coat of lard melted away.
Carrots and gourds, last year's vegetables, partially filled floppy
baskets. I snatched a carrot from one of the baskets and placed the
softening tuber in my pocket. I had learned that meals might not
come regularly, and I was not going to let an opportunity pass to
put food in my stomach.

The lowest shelves hung two handsbreadths off of the floor, and
though I imagined cockroaches or worse made a home under the
shelves, the room was kept clean and free of dirt and dust. This
seemed like the most private place to store my belongings, and
the sleeping mat would fit there as well.

After stashing my effects, I made my way back to the laundry.
The laundress was waiting for me, this time on a broad chair that
had not been present the day before. In the dim light, she looked
like a gargantuan spider placidly appraising her next meal.

"Well, well, the princess awakes. I trust that you slept peace-
fully?"

I said nothing, unsure how to prevent her from pouncing.

"Do you know what we do to encourage punctuality?"

"No, miss." My voice was hardly above a whisper.

"Ten lashes," she said lightly, almost cheerfully. "But in your
case, since you are new, we shall make it only five. I think that
will help you to remember next time. I borrowed this whip from

the stable." She raised her right arm, and I saw the short leather horsewhip uncoil from her hand.

"Turn and lift your dress."

A fire roared to life in my belly. I could take my punishment, but whips are for beasts.

"Hurry, now!" she said sweetly, cocking her head as though she were offering me a treat.

I turned toward the wall. The heat flared, licking around my heart. I held my dress over my head, and when the first blow landed, I was relieved. It was not as heavy as my father's lashes. He would make us cut green switches from a hazel tree in our croft to use for our own beatings. Before that thought was fully formed, burning agony seared my back. Pain tore through my breast, my head, my limbs, dwarfing the heat in my belly. I gasped. Pain still mounted when the second blow landed. Then the third. White light filled my vision even when I closed my eyes. Four. Five. On the fifth lash, I collapsed to my knees.

"Get up," the laundress said evenly.

When I did not move, she said, "I shall have to whip you again if you are slothful as well as tardy."

I rose and lowered my dress as carefully as I could. The fabric scorched my back.

"Take this back to the stable. They may need it for the other animals." She tossed the whip at my feet, and I bent slowly to retrieve it. The pain was beginning to recede, making room for my anger. I walked stiffly, trying to keep the cloth from touching my back.

I was tempted to walk out the door, through the orchards, meadow, and woods, and keep walking all the way home. I was old enough to know, however, that my family could not keep me, and I had nowhere else to go.

In the stable, I found a boy repairing a saddle. He looked up, blinking. The stable seemed smaller in the sunlight than it had in the dark of the rainstorm. I had hoped to find the building unoccupied. My cheeks warmed; I wanted to hide the whip behind my back. Instead, I mumbled, "I am returning this for Miss Elisabeth," and I placed the whip beside him. The boy appeared uninterested; he yawned and resumed his work. Beatings were commonplace.

"Are there horse blankets needing mending?" I asked.

He looked up again. "Sure. There's always blankets in need of mending. Who are you?"

"Agnes. The new laundry girl."

He shrugged. "Don't know why you want to, but the blankets are hanging on the pegs." He motioned with his head. "Take any one. They all have holes."

I selected a blue blanket that appeared newer than the rest, and, without thinking, slung it over my shoulder. I failed to swallow a short cry of pain as the blanket slapped against my back. I slinked away, letting my "Good morning!" trail behind me, where it may have gone unheard.

Before returning to the laundry, I ran to the kitchen to deposit the blanket. The room had become a bustling hub of activity. Menservants busied themselves stirring pots, hanging cauldrons, chopping vegetables, baking bread, crushing spices, straining sauces, feeding the fire. Only the head cook stood still, barking orders that sometimes drowned in bangs, clangs, and crashes as the other servants hustled around him like a stream divided by a rock. Echoes from the vaulted roof amplified the din. The sticky swelter of the kitchen was worsened by the sun's rays streaming through the skylights, and the fires were banked high. Steaming moisture coated the gray stone walls of the vast room. The massive, sagging beam that spanned the breadth of the kitchen seemed to float in the haze; headless pink carcasses dangled from iron hooks screwed into its underside. Near the larder, a man butchered what appeared to be a goat. He leaned on his cleaver, red-faced and sweating, a slash of blood across his tunic. I passed him without being noticed, stashed the horse blanket with my other belongings, and hastened to the laundry.

It did not seem as though the laundress had moved since I left her, but she must have, for she now held a loaf of bread in her tiny, dimpled hand. She tore delicately at the soft-crusted loaf, chewing slowly and deliberately. "I am glad to see that you are learning to be prompt." She paused for another bite. "You will need to start every day by dawn if you expect to keep up with the laundry. As long as you get your work done and don't complain, I shan't have to correct you." She smiled. "You are late today, but you can begin by draining the water from the bucking tub into the laundry pool. Unfortunately, the basin is too dirty to use for dollying, so you will have to clean it first." She brushed crumbs from her lap. "The chamber pots are beside the basin. Pour the piss into the bucket once you are finished hauling water. I shall return the pots."

I wondered why she chose to return the pots. It was amply evident that she intended for me to do all of the work; why would she reserve this task for herself? Perhaps she wanted to see the belongings that the guests left in their chambers. I had overheard the kitchen staff complaining about so many mouths to feed today.

Elisabeth readjusted her bulk in the chair. "If you don't want to be up so late, you had better get busy. You have a lot of catching up to do."

"Yes, miss." I kept my eyes fixed on the wobbling flesh beneath her chin. My back still burned, and my heart was leaden, but I would not let her see me cry.

After the laundress left, I took the flaccid carrot from my pocket and ate it while I planned. If I could manage the bucking at the same time as I worked on the other tasks, it would save time. I needed a clean place to put the laundry from the bucking tub, though, so I would need to scrub the pool first. I cursed the laundress again. If the basin had been in continuous use, it would not be filled with slime. Emptying and refilling the pool would take hours if I had to carry the dirty water one pail at a time all of the way outside.

I looked at the window high in the wall. It was unglazed and loosely shuttered; spiders had weaved a dense curtain of lacy web. If only I could throw the dirty water out of the window, the pool would soon be empty.

I rummaged through the laundry until I had an armful of light stockings and handkerchiefs, and then I tied them securely together in a chain. The bucket handle creaked as I attached it to one end of my improvised rope. It would be difficult to remove the knots later, but I did not mind paying that price if this scheme saved me time.

After placing the bucket in the laundry basin, I climbed carefully onto the bucking tub. Tautening fabric across my back caused me to gasp as I pulled myself up. Bracing my feet against opposite lips of the barrel, I teetered into an upright position. From that vantage point, I could see that the window had a broad sill. It was a long leap, but worth an attempt.

I tied the rope to my wrist so that I would not drop it, and then I jumped from the barrel, grabbing the windowsill with both hands. I used all of the strength in my sore arms to haul myself to the window, my feet scrabbling against the stone wall. The pain in my back was searing, and I scraped my forearms and knees as I struggled to take a seat on the sill. Despite my discomfort, I was pleased with my success. When I knocked the rotting shutters open, the shawl of spiderwebs tore asunder and flapped in ragged streamers in the clean breeze that blew through the west-facing window. I could see the orchards from my perch. The plum trees were in bloom, a girlish blush of rose next to the barren apple trees. Soon those old crones would also cover themselves in pink and white blooms, a brief vanity before bearing fruit.

The sun had just passed its zenith, and I turned my face toward its warming rays, closing my eyes. I could hear the chirrup of a lonely frog. The sun drew bright squiggles on the inside of my eyelids and banished the cold from my bones. My mother was up there, in heaven. I wondered if she saw me. She would probably tell me to get to work.

I tugged on the rope attached to the bucket handle until it tipped over in the basin below. Then, with a swift pull, I lifted the bucket of water toward me. With two hands, I could manage. A green splash sloshed from the bucket as it grated over the sill. Balancing the bucket at the edge of the outer windowsill, I tipped the foul water onto the new grass below. I then lowered the bucket to the basin and drew up another full pail.

The basin was soon empty enough for a good scrubbing. I was about to hop down from the window when John called up to me.

"You really are a mouse, crawling up into the windows! Does Miss Elisabeth know what you are up to?" He set the empty wheelbarrow on its feet and tipped his hat back until I could see his squinting eyes.

I shook my head and placed my finger to my lips, hoping that he would lower his voice.

"Are you coming for dinner? I was just heading in myself. After the master has finished dining, the servants gather in the kitchen. Join us!"

I smiled at him and waved. Food would be very welcome. After jumping down, I emptied some water from the bucking tub into the basin and scrubbed it thoroughly. It would be better to starve than face any more discipline from the laundress. I gave the basin a final rinse and sopped up the dirty wash water with a rag, filling the bucket. I brought the pail with me, planning to discard the water outside on my way to dinner.

Toward the back foyer, the chorus of voices and clatter of dishes from the kitchen grew louder. Hopefully I was not too late for food. I quickened my pace, but just as I crossed the entrance to a short passageway that opened between the buttery and the pantry, an incoherent bellow caused me to freeze. I looked down the dark corridor but saw only a shaft of light from a partly open door that I knew led to the great hall. There was silence for a moment, and then from the depths of the passageway, the rise and fall of a man's voice, ranting, muttering, raging, then muttering again. Realizing that I should not be eavesdropping, I continued toward the kitchen. Before I had taken many steps, the voice roared "Geoffrey!" three times with increasing vehemence, and I heard a door slam with a reverberating bang.

It seemed to me very bad luck that I was alone in the hallway when Geoffrey Poke quickly limped out of the kitchen, scowling, aiming for the corridor by the pantry. He carried a carafe and cups on a tray, and in his haste, one of the cups tottered over the edge and smashed on the stone floor. He cursed, and his scowl deepened

Index

About the Author

Leah Weiss, PhD, is a researcher, professor, consultant, and author. She teaches courses on compassionate leadership at the Stanford Graduate School of Business and is the principal teacher and founding faculty for Stanford's Compassion Cultivation Program, conceived by the Dalai Lama. She also directs compassion education and scholarship at HopeLab, an Omidyar Group research-and-development nonprofit focused on resilience. She lives in Palo Alto, California, with her husband and three children.